PONY❤DAYS

SHELTIE
Races
On

✔ **W9-AWO-487**

Read all the

PONY♥DAYS

books:

PONY♥DAYS

SHELTIE
Races
On

by Peter Clover

Cover illustration by
Tristan Elwell

AN
Apple
PAPERBACK

SCHOLASTIC INC

New York   Toronto   London   Auckland   Sydney
Mexico City   New Delhi   Hong Kong   Buenos Aires

ISBN 0-439-80154-0

Copyright © 2000 by Working Partners Ltd.
Created by Working Partners Ltd, London W6 0QT

12 11 10 9 8 7 6 5 4 3   6 7 8 9 10/0

Printed in the U.S.A.   40

First Scholastic printing, November 2005

To Alan, Lionel, and Bernard

PONY ♥ DAYS

SHELTIE
Races
On

Chapter One

"Sheltie! Bring that back right now!" called Emma. "I'm not finished grooming you yet!"

Sheltie, Emma's sassy little Shetland pony, paid no attention. He flicked his long bushy tail and trotted away with the dandy brush clamped between his teeth.

When he was a safe distance away, Sheltie stopped and turned to face Emma. He dropped the brush on the grass and gave one of his funny snorts, where his

lips went back and his front teeth showed.
Emma giggled to herself. Sheltie always
looked as if he was laughing when he
did that.

"Sheltie! Bring that brush back right
now!" she ordered again.

Emma tried to sound stern, but she

wasn't really angry. The trouble was, Sheltie knew that, too! He looked at Emma through his shaggy forelock and blew her a short, sharp raspberry. Then he deliberately tapped the brush with his front hoof and teased Emma by pushing it toward her.

"OK!" said Emma. "So you want me to come and get it?"

Sheltie answered with a teasing whinny.

"You don't think I'm fast enough, do you?" said Emma, laughing.

The Shetland pony fixed Emma with his big brown eyes as she moved slowly toward him.

Suddenly, Emma made a quick dash forward, but she wasn't *quite* fast enough. Sheltie was ready for her. He ducked his head and snatched the brush off the grass. Then he turned quickly and galloped away with a muffled snort.

Sheltie did a fast lap around his paddock and came up behind Emma in a big circle. He dropped the brush on the grass and wanted to start the game all over again.

"Oh, no!" Emma laughed. "I'm not playing anymore." She started packing the grooming things away in her bag, and watched out of the corner of her eye as Sheltie pushed the brush forward again with his hoof.

"Come on," pleaded Emma. "Be a good boy and bring it back."

Sheltie picked up the brush with his teeth and trotted slowly back to Emma.

"That's a good boy," said Emma. "Now stand still while I finish your mane."

This time Sheltie didn't move. He closed his eyes and waited for Emma to comb out his mane.

"See?" said Emma when she had finished. "You *can* be really good when you want to be." And she gave him a peppermint as a reward.

But minutes later, she was chasing him around the paddock again, trying to get back the currycomb that Sheltie had snatched from out of the bag.

"Morning, Emma," called the mailman from the other side of the fence. "I see Sheltie's keeping you busy, as usual."

Emma stopped running and smiled.

"It's my own fault," she said. "Sheltie wouldn't run off with things if I didn't chase after him!"

"And I bet you *never* catch him," said the

mailman, laughing. "Sheltie goes like a rocket, doesn't he? I don't think I've ever seen a Shetland pony run so fast."

"He thinks he's a racehorse," said Emma with a grin. "No one's ever told him he's just a little pony."

From across the paddock, Sheltie gave a loud snort.

"I think he heard you," joked the mailman. "You'd better take your letter before Sheltie starts chasing *you*."

"*My* letter?" exclaimed Emma. "There's a letter for me?" Her face lit up as the mailman handed her a white envelope.

"I wonder who it's from," said Emma.

"Open it and see." The mailman winked. "But be quick — here comes trouble."

Sheltie was trotting across the grass

toward them to see what was going on. He was looking curiously at the envelope in Emma's hand.

Emma just had time to stuff it under her sweatshirt and hide it from Sheltie before he arrived. The last thing Emma wanted was her mischievous pony eating her letter before she'd had a chance to read it.

"Comb, please," said Emma, holding out her palm. Sheltie dropped the currycomb onto her hand. "Good boy!" she praised, then gave him another minty treat before running into the house to read her letter in peace.

Chapter Two

"I got a letter!" announced Emma as she burst into the kitchen.

"That's exciting," said Mom. "I wonder who it's from."

"The postmark says Rilchester," puzzled Emma. "That's just on the other side of the meadows. I wonder who's written to me from Rilchester. I don't know anyone who lives there!"

"Why don't you open it and find out,

instead of trying to guess who it's from?" said Mom, laughing.

Emma opened the envelope and unfolded the notepaper inside.

"Should I read it to you?" she asked eagerly.

Mom nodded and sat at the kitchen table as Emma began to read.

"Dear Emma,

My name is Carrie Palmer and I live on Barton Farm in Rilchester.

My friend Mrs. Linney told me all about you and Sheltie, your little Shetland pony. You may remember another Shetland pony named Topper. He was a rescued circus pony who now lives with me on the farm.

Mrs. Linney told me that Sheltie and Topper look like identical twins. I would be really interested in teaming Sheltie with Topper to compete in the novelty Roman chariot race at the Greenham Gardens County Show. What do you think?"

Emma stopped for a moment and stared at the letter.

"Wow! This sounds exciting!" she said.

"Sheltie and Topper got along so well together. They'd make a fantastic team!"

"Does it say anything else?" asked Mom.

"Oh, yes," said Emma, and she continued to read.

"If you and Sheltie would like to be part of the Roman Rockets, please call me at 555-6842, and we can discuss a training program."

Emma's eyes opened wide. "Double wow!" she said. "The Roman Rockets *and* a training program! Sheltie's going to love this. Can we do it, Mom? Please can we?" she asked.

A smile spread across Mom's face. "Of course you can," she said. "But I'll just call Carrie Palmer first to check the details."

"And I'll go tell Sheltie right now," piped in Emma.

On her way out, Emma grabbed her little brother Joshua's hand and spun him around.

"Come on, Joshua. Sheltie and I are going to the races." Then she ran with him all the way down to the paddock.

"Races, races," said Joshua, giggling, as his little legs struggled to keep up with Emma's.

Emma and Sheltie watched from the paddock as Mom came out of the house and walked toward them.

"Well, I spoke to Carrie Palmer," said Mom.

"*And?*" asked Emma eagerly.

"And, *yes*, of course you and Sheltie can join the Roman Rockets."

"Great!" said Emma.

"But this novelty race is a serious event, Emma," Mom added. "It's for charity, so you *must* be certain that you want to do it. Carrie's hoping to raise money for a local children's hospital. Lots of her friends have agreed to sponsor the Roman Rockets for taking part in the event."

"I understand," said Emma, "and I *do* want to do it. I really do," she added enthusiastically. "I can't wait to race Sheltie and Topper in a Roman chariot."

"Ah . . ." said Mom quietly.

Emma noticed that Mom was making a funny face.

"I don't think it's going to be *you* doing the racing, Emma," Mom continued. "You'll be more of an assistant . . . a special trainer." She was trying to break the news

14

as gently as she could. "It will be Carrie who actually drives the Roman chariot in the race."

"Oh." Emma sighed, feeling disappointed. But her smile soon returned. "Assistant *and* special trainer! That can't be too bad, can it, Sheltie?" she said.

The little pony tossed his mane with a loud snort, as if to say, "Not bad at all!"

Chapter Three

After school the following day, Carrie
Palmer came over to meet Sheltie and talk
to Emma.

Carrie Palmer was about eighteen, with
long curly red hair and a happy laugh.

"Just call me Carrie," she said with a
smile.

Emma liked Carrie right away. She was
lively and loved horses and ponies.

into the soft straw barriers. They were going too fast.

Emma pulled on the reins and slowed down a little. Sheltie and Topper were amazing — they were perfectly in time with each other, weaving in and out of the barrels, clearing the obstacle course in third place.

Emma flicked the reins again, and the Roman Rockets flew along the track, completing the second lap to loud cheers from the crowd.

The Midnight Flyers were still in the lead as they approached the obstacle course for the second time. Next there was a team of piebald ponies, and then came the Roman Rockets.

The Midnight Flyers were going too fast. Suddenly, they were completely out of control. They hit the obstacle course, scattering barrel after barrel. The team of piebalds dashed forward, missed the turn, and almost tipped their chariot over. But through all the dust and confusion came the Roman Rockets.

"Go, Sheltie, go," yelled Emma as the chariot tore along. "Run, Topper, run."

The Midnight Flyers had recovered now and were close behind, gaining little by little as Emma drove her chariot along the home stretch. Emma could see the glossy black heads of the Dartmoors out of the corner of her eye. With only a few feet to go, she flicked the reins one last time and cried, "Fly, Sheltie! Topper, fly!"

The Roman Rockets crossed the finish line in first place.

"Yes!" screamed Emma. "Yes! We won, we won. Well done, Sheltie. Well done, Topper."

The crowd went wild. Carrie ran to the front with her curly red hair flying in the breeze. She wanted to be the first to congratulate Emma and her team.

"You did it! You did it! Well done, Emma. Well done, Sheltie and Topper! The Roman Rockets have won! It's fantastic."

Mom, Dad, and Joshua joined them.

"You were incredible," said Mom. She gave Emma a huge hug. "I'm so proud of you!"

Emma felt great. It was the best feeling in the world.

But it didn't last long. . . .

After the race came the presentation of the Caesar Cup.

Emma and Carrie unharnessed Sheltie and Topper and led them across to the raised stage. As everyone crowded around the Roman Rockets to pet and stroke the two winning ponies, Emma noticed that the driver of the Midnight Flyers was hanging around near her chariot, just below the stage.

I wonder what he's up to? thought Emma.

Mrs. Greenham was up on stage, taking more photographs of the crowd and the winning team. At last, Mr. Greenham took

the microphone and hushed the excited
crowd. This was the moment that everyone
was waiting for — the presentation of the
prize. But instead of looking happy, Mr.
Greenham looked rather anxious.

"I'm afraid there's some bad news," he began. "The Caesar Cup is missing! We can't find it anywhere."

Everyone looked disappointed. Before Mr. Greenham could continue, a voice spoke up from the crowd. It was the driver of the Midnight Flyers.

"I bet I know who took it," he yelled. "That girl and her ponies are thieves!" He pointed straight at Emma. "She's already been caught trying to steal my grooming brushes," he added. Then he ran across to Emma's chariot and pulled off a cover in the back.

Emma couldn't believe it. There, lying in the back of her chariot, was the Caesar Cup. Just like the boy had said. But how? She had never seen it before.

"Thief!" yelled the nasty boy. "She's a thief and she's been caught red-handed."

Emma felt as though she was about to burst into tears. Sheltie and Topper tossed their heads and snorted loudly. Everyone was looking up at them. It was horrible.

Suddenly, Mrs. Greenham stepped forward.

"I don't think anyone should listen to this boy!" she announced. "I've been watching Emma and the Roman Rockets all morning. And I've been taking lots of photographs, too. She hasn't stolen anything."

"But the Cup's in her chariot," sneered the boy. "That's proof that she stole it. She should be disqualified."

"And I've got film in my camera that proves that she didn't steal it," said Mrs. Greenham. "What it *will* show, though, is a silly boy playing a nasty trick on an innocent girl. It shows *you* putting it there, young man! I saw exactly what you did a few moments ago. And I've got the evidence right here." She tapped her camera.

The boy's face turned very red.

"The Roman Rockets have won fair and square," said Mrs. Greenham. "They were the fastest team in the race."

Everyone in the gardens agreed and a big cheer rang out.

"Emma Matthews and the Roman Rockets have won the Caesar Cup," announced Mr. Greenham. His wife handed him the Cup, which she had retrieved from Emma's chariot. Mr. Greenham presented it to Emma, and Emma held it high in the air.

Sheltie gave a loud whinny, and Topper immediately copied him.

Mrs. Greenham snapped away with her camera and smiled. "That's a lovely one of Sheltie," she said.

"That's not Sheltie," said Emma with a grin. "That's Topper."

"So *this* one is Topper?" asked Mrs. Greenham.

"No," said Emma, laughing. "This is *Sheltie*."

"I really don't know how you can tell them apart," puzzled Mrs. Greenham.

"It's easy," said Emma. "There's only one Sheltie!"

It had been a really exciting day. Emma had *never* expected to be driving the chariot, and she had *never* expected Sheltie and Topper to win the race.

She was just about to ruffle the two ponies' forelocks and go to join Mom and Dad when Sheltie suddenly snatched at the line of flags fastened to the stage.

As quick as a flash, Topper grabbed the other end. The line snapped and all the colored flags became tangled around their necks.

Sheltie lurched forward before Emma had a chance to stop him, and the two Shetland ponies took off together. The Roman Rockets had decided to do an unexpected victory lap around the track!

They looked so funny with the line of flags trailing along behind them that Emma laughed, even though she knew Sheltie and Topper were being naughty. Everyone in the crowd started to laugh, too.

It had turned out to be the best day ever, thanks to Sheltie and his teammate, Topper.

* * *

One week later, Emma was in the paddock, grooming Sheltie.

"Package for Emma Matthews,"
called the mailman, waving a small box
in the air.

"For me?" exclaimed Emma. Sheltie
tossed his mane and tried to snatch the
package as the mailman passed it to Emma
across the paddock fence.

"It's from Rilchester," said Emma. She
quickly tore open the box and pulled out a
beautiful book of photographs.

"Oh, look!" said Emma. She held up the
front cover for Sheltie to see.

On it was a picture of Sheltie and
Topper, identical twins in identical poses.
They stood together, with a line of colorful
flags tangled around their necks.

Inside the book, there were lots of
pictures of the Greenham Gardens County

Show, and lots of pictures of Sheltie and Topper — the Roman Rockets. The very last picture in the book was of Emma holding the Caesar Cup. It brought back lots of memories.

"It was a fantastic day, wasn't it, boy?" said Emma. "And we helped to buy all that equipment for the children's hospital."

Sheltie tilted his head to one side slyly,
then snatched the book from Emma and
ran off across the paddock.

"Oh, you naughty, naughty pony,"
Emma called after him.

But she couldn't help laughing all
the same.

Emma wanted to be just like her when she grew up.

Sheltie came trotting across the paddock to be introduced. Carrie rubbed his hairy ears and ruffled his long shaggy mane.

"Wow, it's amazing!" she exclaimed. "Sheltie looks *exactly* like Topper. They could be twins. And I bet he goes like a rocket, too!"

"Like a Roman rocket," said Emma, grinning. "Would you like to see how fast he can gallop?"

Before Carrie could say anything, Emma clapped her hands and urged Sheltie to dash around the paddock.

"I told you he was fast," said Emma with a laugh as they watched him race by.

Carrie was impressed. "With Sheltie on
the team, the Roman Rockets stand a really
good chance of winning the Caesar Cup."
Sheltie trotted over and blew an impish

raspberry. Then he pushed his muzzle into Emma's hand, looking for a reward. She palmed the little pony a peppermint treat, then looked up at Carrie.

"So when do we start training?" she asked.

"As soon as you can," answered Carrie. "The County Show is only two weeks away, so there's not that much time. And it would be great if you could get some of your friends to sponsor us, too!"

"We can train after school every day," said Emma eagerly. "And next week it's school vacation, so we'll be able to train all day every day for a whole week before the show!"

Sheltie pranced on the spot, pumping his little legs up and down. He seemed to

19

know that something exciting was about to happen.

"Look at Sheltie." Emma laughed. "He wants to start training right away — and he can't wait to see Topper again."

Carrie smiled. "Mrs. Linney tells me that Sheltie has a little fish cart," she said. "Do you think you could show me, Emma?"

"It's behind Sheltie's field shelter, isn't it, boy?" said Emma. "Should we show Carrie?" The little pony pawed at the grass with his hoof, then trotted off, with Emma and Carrie following close behind. When they reached the field shelter, Sheltie was already in place, standing between the shafts of his fish cart.

"It's perfect!" exclaimed Carrie. "It's

smaller than the Roman chariot, but it's
ideal for you to train with."

"What kind of things should I be
teaching Sheltie?" asked Emma. "He's
already very good at pulling the cart
along at a gallop."

"I'd like to see that," said Carrie. "Should we put Sheltie in the harness?"

In no time at all, Emma had harnessed her pony to the shafts of the fish cart. Sheltie flicked his long shaggy tail and waited for Emma to climb into the cart and gather up the reins.

"First I'd like you to trot Sheltie in a straight line down to the end of the paddock," said Carrie. "Then turn him around in a circle and gallop back as fast as you can."

"Sheltie will love that, won't you?" said Emma. The little pony blew through his lips and made a noise like a motorbike revving up.

"Are you ready, boy?" Sheltie bobbed his head up and down, and Emma flicked the reins. "Go, boy! Go!"

The Shetland pony trotted in a perfect straight line down to the end fence. Then Emma turned the cart and urged Sheltie into a gallop. He flew like a real rocket, pulling the fish cart smoothly along behind him.

"That was awesome!" exclaimed Carrie. "Sheltie can really move, can't he?"

"He's the fastest Shetland pony in the world," said Emma with a grin.

"Let's hope he and Topper are fast enough together to win the Cup," said Carrie. "For the last three years we've only ever managed second place — we always lose out to the Midnight Flyers. It's about time we came in first, and I think Sheltie and Topper are going to be the ones to make it happen."

"I know they'll do their best," enthused

Emma. "We'll train really hard and try not to let you down."

"Great!" said Carrie. "It's a good idea to practice as often as you can," she added. "First of all, I want you to keep galloping in straight lines. Then you can set up some obstacles and practice weaving the cart in and out between them."

"We've got some old orange crates in the shed," said Emma. "I sometimes use them to set up jumps. They'll make a good obstacle course."

"They sound perfect," said Carrie. "I'll bring Topper over next Saturday," she added, "and we can pair the ponies together in the real racing chariot. Then we'll see just how good our team really is."

* * *

Emma and Sheltie trained every day after
school.

Emma set up an obstacle course and

practiced steering Sheltie and the cart in and out of the orange crates, just like Carrie had said. They practiced fast turns and quick starts, and they raced up and down the paddock without stopping. Sheltie enjoyed every single minute of it. When Emma came home from school, he would be standing between the shafts of his cart, ready for his training.

By the end of the week, Emma was convinced that Sheltie was the fastest thing on four legs.

Chapter Four

On Saturday morning, Carrie and Topper came over from Rilchester, as planned. Emma and Sheltie watched from the paddock as the big horse trailer backed into their driveway. Painted across the side of the trailer were the words ROMAN ROCKETS.

Emma felt a shiver of excitement. "Do you see that, Sheltie?" she whispered.

The little pony pricked up his ears, listening to Emma's voice.

"The Roman Rockets," she said. "That's us. We're part of the team."

Sheltie threw back his head and blew a loud snort as the trailer crunched to a halt on the gravel.

From inside the trailer came an answering whinny.

Sheltie's ears pricked up again.

"Do you remember Topper?" asked Emma. "He's your teammate. He's come to train with you today."

Sheltie called to his old friend with another snort.

"Hi, Emma. Hello, Sheltie," said Carrie as she stepped down from the cab.

Topper was making a lot of noise inside the trailer, and Sheltie was making even more noise outside.

"These two sound as if they're going to

be really pleased to see each other again," said Carrie. She unlocked the back of the trailer and threw open the door. Then she lowered the ramp and climbed inside.

Moments later, Carrie led Topper down the ramp with a clatter of hooves.

Sheltie blew a raspberry to greet his friend, and Emma stared at the two identical ponies. She had forgotten just how alike they were. She smiled as Sheltie and Topper stretched their necks to rub noses through the wooden rails of the paddock fence.

Emma swung the gate open and Carrie released Topper into the field. The two Shetland ponies galloped off in a wild game of chase.

"It's hard to tell who's chasing who, isn't it?" remarked Carrie.

"I can tell," said Emma confidently.
"That's Topper chasing Sheltie . . . and now
it's Sheltie chasing Topper."

"How do you do it, Emma?" asked Carrie.

Emma grinned. "I'd know Sheltie
anywhere!" she said.

While the two ponies were enjoying their romp, Emma helped Carrie to wheel the Roman chariot out of the trailer and into the paddock. It wasn't much bigger than Sheltie's fish cart, but it had enormous wheels and was painted bright red. Like the trailer, the sides of the chariot bore the words ROMAN ROCKETS written in gold letters.

"If you hold the center pole clear of the ground, Emma, I'll wheel it through from behind," suggested Carrie.

Emma felt really proud as she led the chariot through.

Carrie showed Emma the two leather harnesses that Sheltie and Topper would wear and explained how they fastened to the center pole of the chariot.

"Since Sheltie and Topper are both used

to wearing harness tack and pulling carts,"
said Carrie, "all we have to do is get them
to work together."

"As a team," added Emma.

Carrie smiled, then blew two sharp
blasts on her whistle.

Topper answered the call immediately
and came trotting across the paddock.

Emma was impressed. Carrie had
obviously been working hard with the
little pony.

Emma pursed her lips and whistled, too.
She was eager to show how well trained
Sheltie was. "Here, boy," she called.

Sheltie tossed his mane and his eyes
twinkled brightly beneath his forelock.
Then he trotted quickly across the grass
to Emma.

"*Yes!*" she whispered. "Good boy,
Sheltie."

She gave each pony a peppermint treat.
They munched them greedily, then stood
side by side, like naughty twins, hoping
they might get another one.

Chapter Five

Harnessing Sheltie and Topper to the chariot wasn't quite as easy as Emma thought it would be.

The two ponies kept fooling around and showing off in front of each other.

But Emma wasn't going to stand for any nonsense. "There'll be no more treats if you both misbehave," she warned sternly. Sheltie blew a rude raspberry and gave himself the hiccups.

"Serves you right," said Emma as she finally fixed his harness to the chariot.

"I can see that Sheltie and Topper are no match for you, Emma," said Carrie, laughing.

She showed Emma how to fit the special bridles on the two ponies and how to organize the long reins. Then she climbed into the chariot.

"Come stand next to me," she said.

Emma didn't waste a second. She took her place next to Carrie and glanced up toward the house. She could see Mom and Joshua watching, and gave them both a little wave. Then she concentrated on what Carrie was showing her.

"It's very similar to driving Sheltie's fish cart," began Carrie. "Only this time there are two ponies and two sets of reins. Watch

how I use the reins to control each pony
separately."

They went for a slow ride around the
paddock. Sheltie and Topper walked
happily along, side by side. Emma was
surprised that they were so well behaved.

Next they tried a trot. Eight little legs pumped in step and pulled the chariot smoothly across the grass.

But Emma thought that the gallop was the best part. At first Sheltie and Topper were out of rhythm, but Carrie was an expert driver and soon had them working as a perfect team, galloping together.

The Roman Rockets flew around the paddock circuit, churning up clods of grass with their pounding hooves.

"This is amazing!" called Emma. "It's fantastic!"

"That's because our two ponies are fantastic," said Carrie. "They need a little work, but I think we've got the makings of a winning team. Those Midnight Flyers had better watch out!"

"Do you think I could have a turn driving?" asked Emma. "I'd really like to try."

"Of course!" said Carrie, smiling.

But as soon as Emma took the reins, the two Shetlands decided to misbehave. It was as if they knew that Carrie was no longer in charge.

First they wouldn't start. Then they wouldn't stop. And then they kept stopping and starting at different times, and bobbing their heads down to snack on patches of clover.

"You'll get used to it soon," encouraged Carrie. "And they'll get used to you, too."

The County Show was only one week away, and suddenly, Emma felt very relieved that Carrie would be driving the chariot in the big race. It wasn't quite as easy as it looked.

Carrie had arranged for Topper to board with Sheltie for the week before the show so that Emma could train the two ponies together every day.

Emma's driving steadily improved as the days went by, but Sheltie and Topper still tried to misbehave when she took up the reins.

When Emma wasn't busy practicing for the race, she drove the chariot through the village, handing out leaflets and asking her friends to sponsor the Roman Rockets.

Emma loved training Sheltie and Topper. She felt like a Roman gladiator, racing her chariot at the Colosseum. She knew all about the Colosseum because she was doing a project on Rome at school.

Sheltie and Topper seemed to be enjoying the training, too. It was like a big game to them. By the end of the week, Emma felt sure that the Roman Rockets were ready for anything — even the Midnight Flyers.

But on the morning of the show, she was feeling a little nervous.

"I've got butterlies in my stomach," she told Mom at breakfast.

"Butterbyes," said Joshua, trying to copy Emma.

Joshua seemed to think that his big sister had eaten butterflies, and now he

wanted some, too, instead of his
cornflakes.

Emma laughed so much she gave herself
hiccups. But at least it made her forget her
nerves.

Chapter Six

At last, the Roman Rockets were on their
way to the County Show.

Once Emma and Carrie had arrived at
Greenham Gardens and Carrie had
parked the trailer near the racetrack,
they set to work getting Sheltie and
Topper ready.

Emma looked around and felt a thrill of
excitement. Lots of other trailers were
parked near them. There were ponies of

all shapes, sizes, and colors — bays, browns, blacks, grays, chestnuts, and roans; Exmoors, Welsh Highlands, Dartmoors, rough Fell ponies, and lots of cross-breeds, too.

But there are only two Shetlands, thought Emma. Sheltie and Topper, the Roman Rockets.

All of the other drivers and their assistants were busy getting their teams ready, too. Brightly colored carts and fancy chariots stood alongside the trailers. Their paintwork gleamed in the morning sunshine. Stalls selling handicrafts and sideshows offering prizes stood side by side on the garden lawns.

"You and Topper will do your very best to win the Caesar Cup today, won't you, Sheltie?" said Emma, suddenly feeling worried that Sheltie and Topper might goof off.

Sheltie blew a mischievous raspberry and shook out his freshly combed mane. Then he nudged his teammate with his muzzle, as if to say, "Of course we will, won't we, Topper?"

The two Shetlands looked their very best, with bouncy manes and bushy tails. Their eyes twinkled beneath their floppy forelocks and their hooves shone with fresh hoof oil.

But as Emma looked around at some of the other ponies, she realized how polished the competition looked — especially the two glossy black Dartmoors being groomed by a boy at the next trailer.

Sheltie and Topper still had their winter

coats and would look quite woolly for another month. They would never be as sleek as some of the others, but they *could* still win the race.

Carrie checked her watch. "Will you be all right finishing on your own while I go register with the race marshalls?" she asked.

Emma puffed out her chest proudly as she slipped off Sheltie's halter.

"Of course I'll be all right," she said, grinning.

"I won't be long," called Carrie, setting off toward the marshalls' tent.

Emma sponged Sheltie's face, then started to clear the grooming things away, packing all the brushes, rags, sponges, and combs into her bag. Sheltie started helping by picking things up, too.

"What a smart pony!" praised Emma. Then Topper joined in and started to copy Sheltie. He picked up the brushes that Sheltie brought him and dropped them into the bag.

"Well done, Topper," said Emma. Then she looked puzzled. . . . Suddenly, Emma realized that she had more brushes than she had started with.

Sheltie must have picked up three brushes from the neighboring trailer, and Topper must have dropped them into Emma's bag!

"Oh! You naughty ponies," she said, laughing when she realized what had happened. She wasn't really annoyed because she knew that Sheltie and Topper were only trying to help.

But before Emma had a chance to return

the brushes, someone started to yell at her
from the next trailer.

"Hey! You!" It was the boy who had
been grooming the two black Dartmoor
ponies. He was much bigger than Emma
and he didn't sound very friendly at all.
"Those scruffy ponies of yours have taken

my best brushes. Give them back at once or I'll report you."

Emma was shocked.

"I'm sorry," she said anxiously. "Sheltie and Topper didn't mean to take your brushes. They were just helping me to clean up."

"That's a good trick," said the boy nastily. "You train ponies to steal things for you and then say it's all a mistake when you get caught."

Emma could see that there was no point in arguing. The boy was never going to believe *anything* she said.

Emma handed over the three brushes and apologized again. "It wasn't a trick at all," she said. "It was just Sheltie and Topper making a mistake."

"Huh!" sneered the boy. "I don't know

what you think you're doing here, anyway, with those two hairy fleabags. You'll never win in a million years. *We* always win everything every year — me and my big brother. We're the Midnight Flyers."

He gave a horrible laugh, snatched back the brushes, and walked away.

"Oh, no!" muttered Emma under her breath. "The Midnight Flyers. I should have known."

Topper blew a loud snort after him. Then Sheltie blew an even louder raspberry and pushed his head into Emma's arms for a hug.

Emma was really upset. The boy's words had been so unfair. She buried her face in Sheltie's soft mane and felt glad that *she* wasn't going to be the one racing against the horrible Midnight Flyers.

"Carrie will show them just how good we are, boy," she whispered to Sheltie. "Carrie will soon wipe the sneer off that mean boy's face."

But Carrie had been gone for ages now. Just as Emma was beginning to worry, she spotted her friend walking toward her, looking worried and upset.

Something terrible had happened. Carrie didn't look as if she would be racing anywhere now. Her arm was in a sling and her wrist was heavily bandaged.

"What happened, Carrie?" cried Emma.

Chapter Seven

Emma ran up to Carrie.

Sheltie cocked his head to one side and watched as Topper sniffed at the white sling.

"I tripped," explained Carrie. "Just as I was stepping into the marshalls' tent to register. I put my hand out to break my fall and I sprained my wrist."

"Oh, no!" cried Emma.

"Luckily, it's not broken," said Carrie.

"But I won't be able to drive the chariot in the big race."

"I guess that means we'll have to pull out of the event." Emma sighed, looking really disappointed.

"Certainly not," said Carrie firmly. "I

registered the Roman Rockets in the name of our second driver."

"Second driver?" asked Emma. "Who's that?"

"Emma Matthews," announced Carrie. "That's who."

"Me?" Emma gasped. "*I* can't do it. I can't race the chariot. I'm not good enough."

"Yes you are," insisted Carrie. "We've waited three years for an opportunity to beat the Midnight Flyers and win the Caesar Cup! We can't let down all the people who sponsored us — and the hospital really needs the equipment we've promised them."

Suddenly, Emma's legs felt wobbly.

"Don't worry, you'll be fine," Carrie reassured her. "You've got two great ponies and you've had plenty of practice. You really *are* a good driver."

"But I'm not *you*," said Emma.

"No." Carrie smiled. "You're Emma Matthews. And you're driving Sheltie and Topper — the Roman Rockets!"

Two hours later, the grounds of Greenham Gardens were crowded with people, and the stalls and sideshows were very busy.

Emma led Sheltie and Topper around in their fancy halters, and lots of people stopped to admire the two ponies.

Suddenly, Sheltie became very interested in a stall selling homemade pies, cakes, and cookies. He poked his nose between two customers and tried to snatch a chocolate cookie.

"No!" scolded Emma, pulling Sheltie away. But as she concentrated on her naughty pony, Topper quickly lunged forward and helped himself to a cupcake.

"Topper!" cried Emma. "You bad boy." Topper paid no attention to Emma and munched happily on his prize while Sheltie licked the crumbs off his friend's muzzle.

Suddenly, Emma noticed the nasty boy from the Midnight Flyers watching her.

"I'm sorry," apologized Emma nervously to the stall-holder.

She expected the stall-holder to be angry, but the jolly woman just laughed.

"What mischievous ponies," she said. "Are they twins?"

"No," answered Emma. "They look alike, but they're just friends."

"Well, I've never seen such identical ponies," said the woman. "Double trouble and handfuls of fun, I bet!" She handed Emma two apples. "Here, give them both a healthy treat later on."

"Thank you," said Emma, grinning as she took the present. But Sheltie and Topper were already pulling her away to the cotton candy stall.

"Come on, you two," said Emma, leading them away. "We'd better go back and get ready for the race."

Emma's mom and dad had arrived with little Joshua. They had found themselves seats in the front row, near the finish line. Emma gave them a wave, then rushed over to tell them all about the change of driver.

"That's fantastic," said Mom.

But Emma wasn't so sure. She hadn't told anyone about her meeting with the boy from the Midnight Flyers. He made her feel nervous, and the thought of racing in front of all those people made butterflies dance in her stomach again.

"Butterbyes!" said Joshua.

"Yes, butterbyes," said Emma, laughing.

There were more than thirty carts and chariots entered in the big race. That was too many for everyone to race together, so there were going to be three heats. In each heat, the first three chariots past the finish line would go through to the final.

The Roman Rockets were in the first heat . . . and so were the Midnight Flyers.

"Good boy, Sheltie," whispered Emma. "Good boy, Topper." She stroked the two ponies as she waited anxiously for the first lineup to be called.

Sheltie nuzzled Emma's arm as she stroked his face.

"Just remember," said Emma, "all we can do is our best." The two ponies blew identical snorts and rippled their rubbery lips.

"You might as well go home now," said a snooty voice. "Or are you still looking for more brushes to steal?" Emma turned around to face the driver of the Midnight Flyers, who had pulled up beside her in his chariot. His glossy black ponies made Sheltie and Topper look really small and scruffy.

"Look," said Emma, "we didn't steal anything, so you should stop saying that we did."

"Why?" sneered the boy.

"Because . . . because it's not fair," complained Emma.

"Oh, you *poor* thing," mocked the boy. "Anyway, I think silly girls with stupid little ponies shouldn't be allowed to enter races that they can't possibly win."

Emma felt her face burning red. She was very angry now, and more determined to win than ever.

Chapter Eight

The race was about to begin. Emma was
at the starting post, reins in her hand.
Sheltie and Topper were jangling their
bits and pawing the ground. They were
raring to go!

The starting pistol fired and the chariots
were off, racing ahead in a thundering
clatter of hooves and wheels. They sped
around the track in a cloud of dust. Sheltie
and Topper flew like the wind as a perfect

team, but they couldn't catch up with the Midnight Flyers. Emma was nervous about the turns, and as they raced toward the finish line, there were four chariots in front of her. She flicked the reins and urged Sheltie and Topper to go even faster. They overtook two chariots, but not the Midnight Flyers. Up ahead she could see the rival team crossing the line in first place.

Emma and the Roman Rockets came in third. But at least they were through to the final.

Sheltie and Topper were blowing hard as Emma steered them back to the waiting enclosure.

"That was fanstastic," said Carrie, ruffling both ponies' manes.

"But we only came in third," said Emma. "The Midnight Flyers won by miles."

"That doesn't matter," said Carrie. "It will be different in the final with the obstacle course. Speed up your turns and make sure Sheltie and Topper work together. You'll sail through."

But will we win? thought Emma. So much was depending on her.

Sheltie threw back his head and gave a loud whinny.

"Well, Sheltie thinks you can do it," said Carrie, laughing.

"I don't know why you're still here," said the driver of the Midnight Flyers. He had drawn his chariot up behind Emma's as she watched the second heat with Sheltie and Topper. "You've already lost once. Do you really want to lose again?"

Emma tried not to listen to him.

"Why don't you just go home?" he continued.

Emma couldn't bear it any longer. She had to say something.

"We're here to do our best," said Emma. "Even if we *do* come in third — or last — at least we'll have tried our hardest."

The boy obviously didn't like Emma standing up to him. Suddenly, he gave his reins a quick flick and made one of his black ponies kick out. The pony's heavy hoof hit Sheltie on the hind leg. Poor Sheltie snorted with fright and pain.

"You did that on purpose!" cried Emma,

jumping out of the chariot to see if Sheltie was all right.

"It was an accident," said the boy sarcastically. "A mistake — like stealing someone's brushes."

Topper tried to lunge at the boy and nip his backside, but he missed.

Emma checked Sheltie's leg and rubbed it gently. The little pony was all right, but his leg was a little sore.

"Come on, boy. We'll wait over there." Emma didn't want to be anywhere near the Midnight Flyers. She even thought about missing the final race, but she knew that she couldn't disappoint Carrie — or the children's hospital.

Instead, she led the chariot across to wait by one of the tents.

"What an attractive-looking team," said a friendly voice. "The Roman Rockets — I like that. Would you mind if I took your photograph?"

Emma looked up into the smiling face of a friendly-looking gray-haired woman. "My name's Mrs. Greenham," she said. "What's yours?"

Emma grinned. "I'm Emma. This is Sheltie and that's Topper."

Mrs. Greenham took a snapshot of the three of them. "I take photographs of the show every year," she said. "I put all of the best ones into a little book, then I have the book printed and we sell souvenir copies to visitors who come to the gardens."

Mrs. Greenham held up her camera again to take another photo, and Sheltie and Topper posed beautifully for her.

Suddenly, Emma realized who Mrs. Greenham was.

"Are you the lady who owns the gardens?" asked Emma.

"That's right," said Mrs. Greenham. "We hold the County Show here every year — to help raise money for local charities."

Emma told Mrs. Greenham how the Roman Rockets were hoping to buy equipment for the children's hospital.

Mrs. Greenham seemed really interested, and before she knew it, Emma found herself talking about her problems with the Midnight Flyers.

"Come with me," said the friendly woman. "I want to show you something."

Sheltie blew a snort and trotted along with Topper as Emma drove the chariot toward a big statue in the gardens. The

statue was of another chariot being pulled
by two warhorses. Driving the chariot was
a fierce-looking young woman.

"Do you know who that is?" asked Mrs.
Greenham.

Emma looked up at the statue and shook her head.

"That's Queen Boadicea," said Mrs. Greenham. "She was a very brave queen who led her army against the Roman invasion in Britain thousands of years ago. Boadicea didn't let *anyone* stand in her way or push her around."

Suddenly, the loudspeakers crackled to life and a voice called all chariot teams in the final heat to report to the starting line.

"Thank you," said Emma. "I'm not afraid anymore. I'm going to compete in the race and do my best! Just like Queen Boadicea." She flicked the reins, and Sheltie and Topper took her to their place alongside the Midnight Flyers.

The two Shetland ponies looked very small next to all of the other ponies. But

Emma didn't care. They were the Roman Rockets. And she was Queen Boadicea!

Emma could see Carrie in the crowd with Mom, Dad, and Joshua. She gave them a big wave. Then she concentrated hard on what the marshall was saying.

"You must complete one lap of the track before weaving your way through the obstacle course," he explained. "Then you do another lap, go through the course again, and finally race to the finish line."

Emma felt Joshua's "butterbyes" fluttering in her stomach. She took a deep breath.

Sheltie and Topper were both pumping their legs eagerly.

"Ready . . . set . . ." *Bang*. The pistol fired and Emma flicked the long reins across the ponies' backs.

"Run, Rockets, run," called Emma, and Sheltie and Topper shot away.

They flew like the wind. And this time Emma wasn't worried about the Midnight Flyers or the fast turns. She was Queen Boadicea, racing for a prize . . . racing for the Caesar Cup.

Chapter Nine

Nine chariots thundered around the racetrack. Nine chariots were racing for the same prize. Sheltie and Topper galloped as fast as their little legs could carry them, but they weren't up at the front with the leaders. The Roman Rockets had a lot of catching up to do if they wanted to win.

The obstacle course loomed before them. Several chariots skidded and crashed